This Little Tiger book belongs to:

_____

_____

_____

For Sarah and Paul
J.S.

For David Moss, Peter,
Mum and Dad
T.L.

First published in Great Britain 1996
This edition published 2003
LITTLE TIGER PRESS
An imprint of Magi Publications
1 The Coda Centre, 189 Munster Road, London SW6 6AW
www.littletigerpress.com
Text © Julie Sykes 1996
Illustrations © Tanya Linch 1996
Julie Sykes and Tanya Linch have asserted their rights
to be identified as the author and illustrator of this work
under the Copyright, Designs and Patents Act, 1988.
A CIP catalogue record for this book
is available from the British Library
ISBN 1 85430 916 1
Printed in Singapore
1 2 3 4 5 6 7 8 9 10

This That

Julie Sykes ... Linch

LITTLE TIGER PRESS
London

Down on the farm Cat woke early.
It was a special day
and she had work to do.

Horse was grazing in the field
when Cat jumped on to the fence.

"Hello, Horse," said Cat. "May I borrow your stable?"
Horse didn't use his stable in the summer because
he liked to sleep outside.
"Yes," he neighed. "What will you use it for?"
"This and that," purred Cat.

Pig was rolling in his sty
when Cat leapt on to the wall.

'Hello, Pig," said Cat. "May I have some of your straw?"
The farmer had just made Pig's bed.
The straw was clean and fresh and there
was plenty of it.
"Help yourself," grunted Pig. "What's it for?"
"This and that," purred Cat.

Goat was playing in the yard
when Cat hopped on the gate and miaowed.

"Hello, Goat," said Cat.
"May I have some hay?"
Goat never ate hay in the
summer when the grass was green and lush.
"If you want," he cried. "Whatever do you
need it for?"
"This and that," purred Cat.

Sheep was dozing under a leafy tree
when Cat climbed on to a branch.

"Hello, Sheep," said Cat. "May I have some
of your soft wool?"
Sheep had a thick white coat and she had
plenty to spare.
"Of course you may," she bleated. "What
are you going to do with it?"
"This and that," purred Cat.

Hen was scratching for grain
when Cat leapt on top of the hen house.

"Hello, Hen," said Cat.
"May I have a few of
your feathers?"
Hen stopped scratching and
cocked her head curiously.
"You may," she clucked.
"But whatever for?"
"This and that," purred Cat.

Cow was drinking from the stream
when Cat joined her on the bank.

"Hello, Cow," said Cat. "May I have a few hairs from your tail?"
Cow had a long tail with a hairy tip for swotting flies.
"Yes," she mooed. "What are you going to do with them?"
"This and that," purred Cat.

Donkey was looking for thistles
when Cat jumped on his back.

"Hello, Donkey," said Cat.

"May I borrow that lovely purple ribbon from your hat?"

Donkey wore a hat to keep the sun out of his eyes.

It was decorated with a bright purple ribbon round the brim.

"If you're careful with it," he said. "What do you want it for?"

"This and that," purred Cat.

The animals thought Cat was behaving strangely.
"What does she want with all our things?" clucked Hen.
"Perhaps she's moving house," mooed Cow.
"No," grunted Pig. "Cats don't like moving."
"Let's follow her," brayed Donkey.

The animals all
hid in the yard,
and when Cat
appeared they
tiptoed after her.

Cat went inside the stable
and the animals followed silently behind.

In one corner they saw . . .

. . . two little kittens.

They were inside a nest
made from hay and straw.
It was lined with
Sheep's wool, hair from
Cow's tail and feathers
from Hen.
It was decorated with
Donkey's pretty purple
ribbon.

"What a lovely surprise,"
neighed Horse.
"They're beautiful," said Goat.
"So that's what you needed our
things for!" exclaimed Sheep.
Leaning over the huge nest,
Donkey asked, "What are
they called?"
Cat sighed. "I don't know, I can't
decide. What do you think?"
The animals looked at each other.

Then together they

neighed and grunted,

bleated and clucked,

hee-hawed and mooed,

"WE KNOW . . .

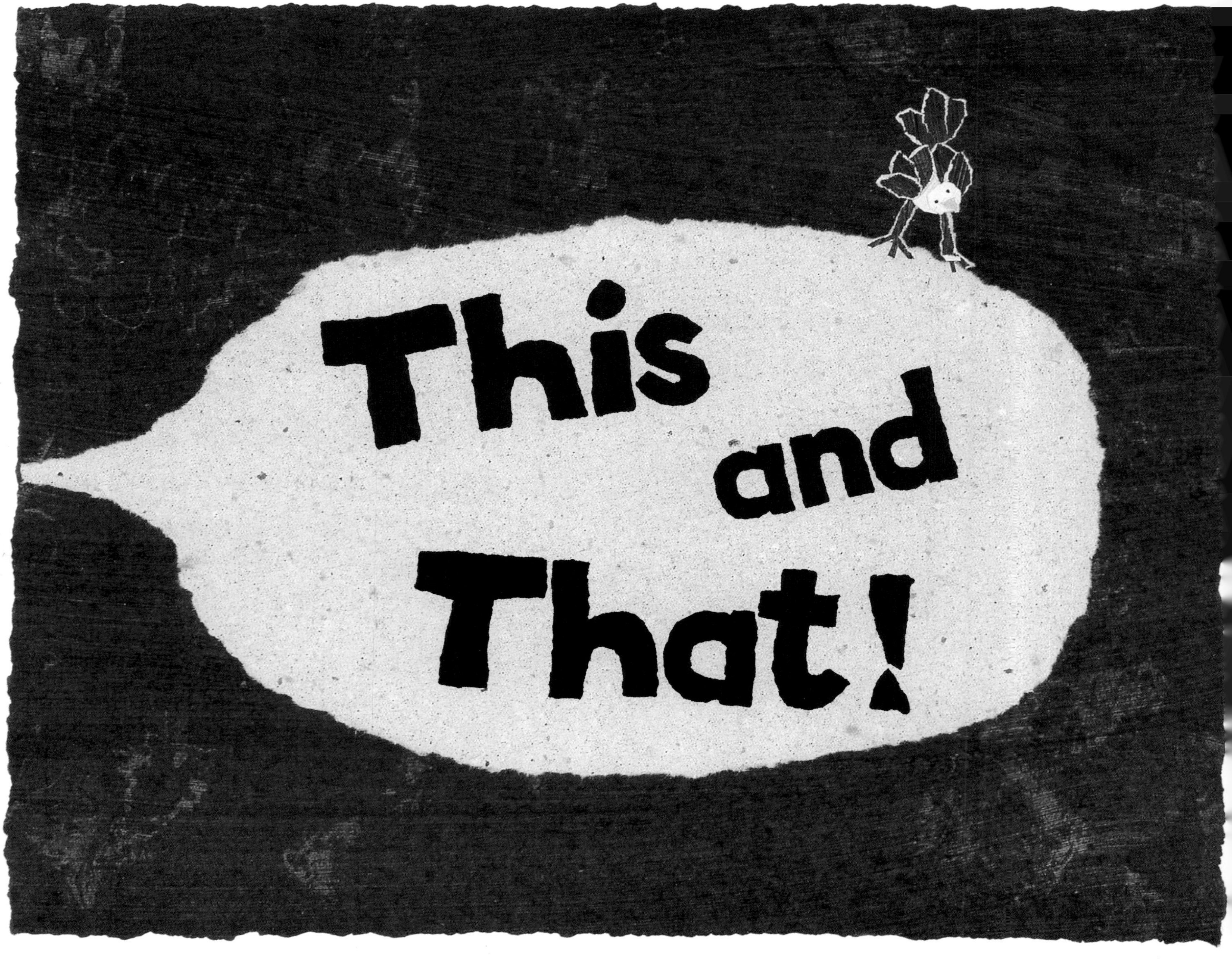
This and That!

More books to curl up with from Little Tiger Press

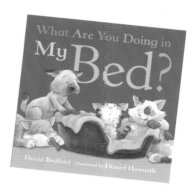

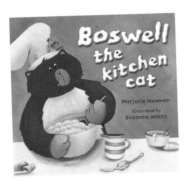

For information regarding any of the above
titles or for our catalogue, please contact us:
Little Tiger Press, 1 The Coda Centre,
189 Munster Road, London SW6 6AW, UK
Tel: 020 7385 6333 • Fax: 020 7385 7333
e-mail: info@littletiger.co.uk
www.littletigerpress.com